Jane Yolen

What to Do with a String

illustrated by

C.F. Payne

designed by Rita Marshall

Creative ✦ Editions

A string, a string
is a marvelous thing.

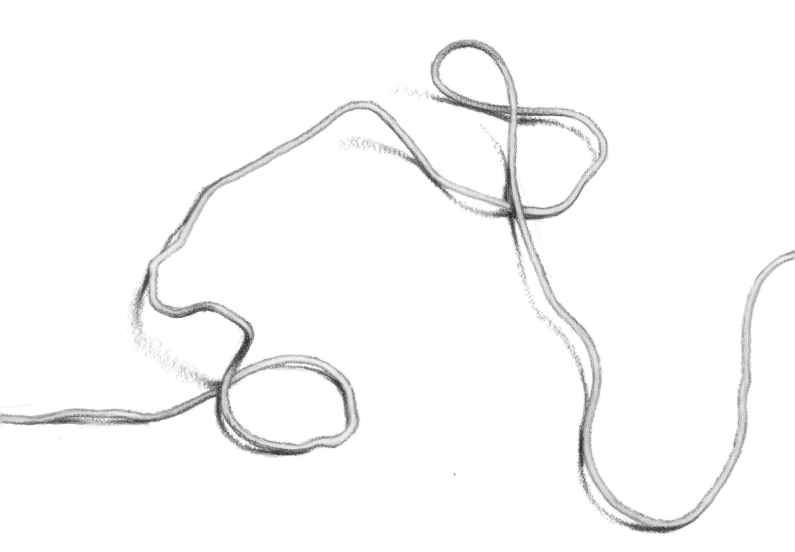

You can curl it
or whirl it,
or twirl it just so.
A string is a toy that
    you never let go.

A string, a string
is a flexible thing,

a lasso that rounds up
some rhinos or moose.

You can weave a strong fence
where they all can run loose.

Or make a big slingshot.

catch mighty *T. rex*,
with his terrible teeth
and his big, awesome pecs.

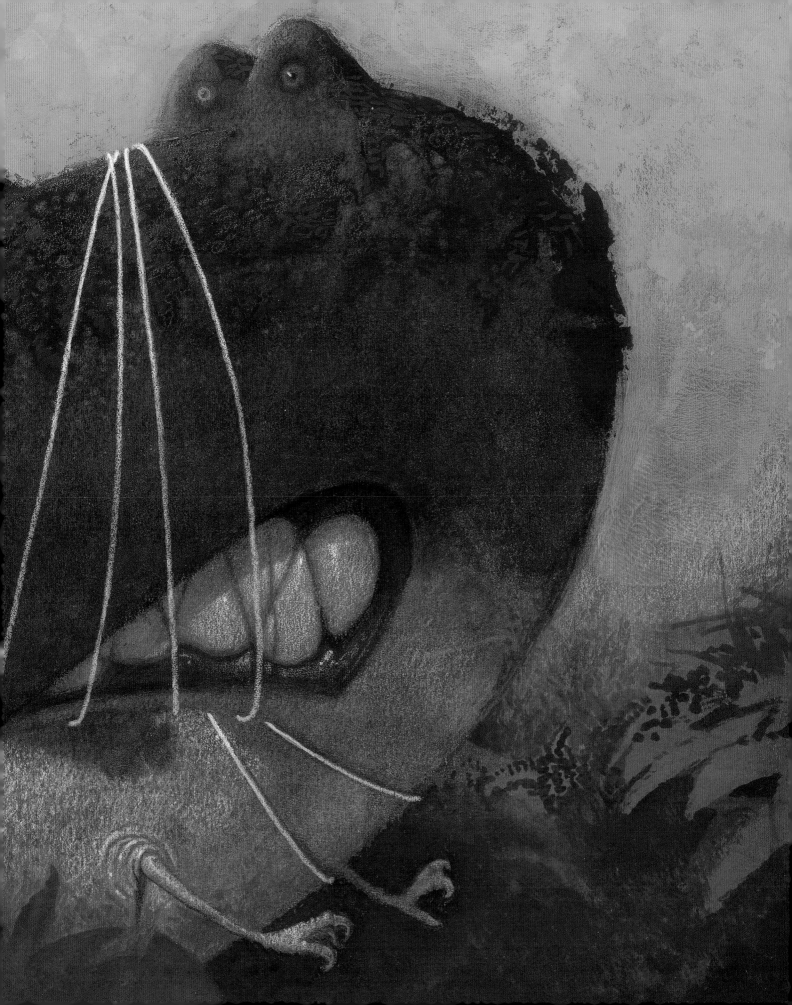

A string, a string
is a braid-able thing.
You can use it to create
a glorious swing.

Or if flight is too scary,
a line for a kite.

so you can stay grounded
and keep that line tight.

You can hang up
a hammock
in the hold of a boat.

Or pull up a sail
so the boat stays afloat.

Or if there's a gale,
hitch a ride on a whale.

Or string up a flag
with a crossbones and skull.

if things at your house
are incredibly dull.

But, if you're still bored,
why, I'll twine a string phone,
and I'll call you,
'cause then

you won't feel so alone.

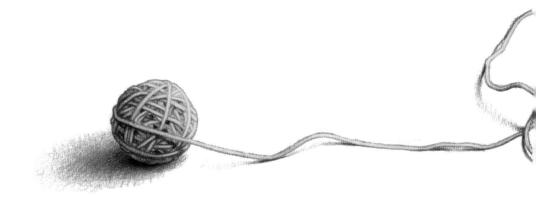

Text copyright © 2019 by Jane Yolen   Illustrations copyright © 2019 by C. F. Payne
Edited by Kate Riggs & Amy Novesky   Published in 2019 by Creative Editions
P.O. Box 227, Mankato, MN 56002 USA
Creative Editions is an imprint of The Creative Company
www.thecreativecompany.us
Library of Congress Cataloging-in-Publication Data
Names: Yolen, Jane, author. / Payne, C. F., illustrator.
Title: What to do with a string / by Jane Yolen; illustrated by C. F. Payne.
Summary: In this sequel to *What to Do with a Box*,
Jane Yolen extolls the marvelous virtues of string,
a material that can snag the spirit of adventure, lasso the
limitless horizons of imagination, and connect us to one another.
Identifiers: LCCN 2018054994 / ISBN 978-1-56846-322-3
Subjects: CYAC: Stories in rhyme. / String-Fiction. / Imagination-Fiction. / Play-Fiction.
Classification: LCC PZ8.3.Y76 Wgm 2019   DDC [E]-dc23
9 8 7 6 5 4 3 2